Disney · PIXAR

BRAVE

Read-Along
STORYBOOK AND CD

It's not so easy being a princess. Or at least not for Merida, who would rather practice archery than learn to curtsy. To find out how this princess's one wish could change her kingdom forever, read along with me in your book. You will know it's time to turn the page when you hear this sound. . . .

Let's begin now.

Printed in the United States of America

3 5 7 9 10 8 6 4

V381-8386-5-12320

ISBN 978-1-4231-3770-2

For more Disney Press fun, visit www.disneybooks.com

DISNEY PRESS

New York

SUSTAINABLE FORESTRY INITIATIVE

Certified Chain of Custody
35% Certified Forest Content,
65% Certified Sourcing
www.sfiprogram.org
SFI-00993

Long ago, there was a kingdom called DunBroch. It was a fierce, proud land. The kingdom was ruled by King Fergus, who was strong and brave, and Queen Elinor, who was wise and fair. King Fergus had lost his leg in a fight with a demon bear named Mor'du. The king swore that one day he would defeat the bear once and for all.

The king and queen had triplet sons and a daughter named Merida. Merida would eventually be queen, and her mother wanted to make sure that the princess was prepared. "A princess must be knowledgeable about her kingdom. Above all, a princess strives for . . . perfection."

Merida did *not* like her mother's rules. What she *did* like was riding full speed through the countryside on her horse, Angus, shooting arrows with her bow. She was very skilled at archery.

One evening, the queen received exciting news from the clans of Macintosh, MacGuffin, and Dingwall. She told Merida that the firstborn from each clan would compete in the palace games. The princess would marry the winner.

Merida was horrified. *Marriage?* "I won't go through with it!" She stormed out of the room.

Queen Elinor followed Merida. She told the princess a story about an ancient kingdom whose king divided the land among his four sons. But one prince wanted to rule the kingdom by himself. He followed his own path, and the kingdom fell apart.

The queen looked at her daughter. "Legends are lessons. They ring with truths."

Despite Merida's protests, the clans arrived. Merida was allowed to decide what their challenge would be. Suddenly, she had an idea. "I choose archery."

After Young Macintosh, Young MacGuffin, and Wee Dingwall had taken their turns with their bows, a hooded figure appeared. "I am Merida, firstborn descendant of clan DunBroch. And I'll be shooting for my own hand!" Merida shot one bull's-eye after another.

Queen Elinor was furious. She took Merida into the castle. Merida glared at her mother. "This whole marriage is what *you* want. Do you ever bother to ask what *I* want? I'm not going to be like you." She turned to the family tapestry hanging on the wall and slashed it with her sword. Then she ran out of the castle and jumped onto her horse.

Merida and Angus galloped through the forest, but suddenly the horse stopped short. They were in the middle of a circle of stones. A strange, glowing blue light appeared.

Merida followed it to a cottage. She opened the door and saw an old woman. When Merida realized that the woman was a witch, she begged for a spell.

The witch told Merida that long ago she had met a prince. He demanded a spell that would give him the strength of ten men.

That was all Merida needed to hear. "Then that's what I want. I want a spell that changes my mother. That will change my fate."

The witch began throwing things into a cauldron. It bubbled and exploded. The witch pulled out a dainty cake.

Merida went home and gave the cake to her mother. "It's a peace offering."

The queen smiled, glad her daughter had returned. She tried the cake, but nothing happened.

Then, as the two walked down the hallway, Queen Elinor stumbled. "Oh. Suddenly, I'm not so well."

Merida put her mother to bed and sat by her side. After a few moments, the queen stood up. As the sheet fell away from her, there, in front of Merida, stood a . . .

"B-B-B-B-B-Bear!"

Merida couldn't believe her eyes. Her mother was a bear! Merida knew she had to get her mother out of the castle. If the king saw a bear, he would surely kill it.

Meanwhile, the triplets had found the spell cake. They gobbled it up—and suddenly, they, too, started to feel a bit strange.

Merida and Queen Elinor raced to the woods. They needed to reverse the spell, but night had fallen, so they took shelter.

The next morning, Merida showed her mother how to catch fish in a stream. For the first time in a while, they had fun together.

Finally, the pair found the witch's cottage. But no one was there. Merida jumped—a voice was coming from the witch's cauldron! It told her: fate be changed, look inside, mend the bond torn by pride.

Then the same blue light appeared. It led them deeper into the woods, to a crumbling ruin.

Merida looked around in confusion. Suddenly, the ground gave way underneath her.

The princess landed in an ancient throne room. There she saw a stone tablet with four princes. One of them had been broken off. Merida gasped. The prince in her mother's story and the one in the witch's story were the same!

Merida looked around.
There were bones on the floor
and claw marks on the walls.
The princess gulped. "Oh,
no. The prince became . . .
Mor'du!" She turned and saw
the evil bear behind her.

Merida barely escaped Mor'du. She and Queen Elinor ran like the wind through the woods.

Merida knew that if they didn't reverse the spell soon, the queen could remain a bear forever, like the prince. She remembered the witch's words. "'Mend the bond torn by pride....' We have to get back to the castle! I know what to do. It's the tapestry!"

In the castle, they found the clans in the middle of a huge battle.

King Fergus was furious. "None of your sons are fit to marry my daughter!"

Lord Dingwall did not like that. "Then our alliance is over! This means war!"

Merida realized that she needed to stop the fighting and decide who she would marry. She faced the crowd. "Our clans were once enemies. But when invaders threatened us from the sea, you joined together to defend our lands. It was an alliance forged in bravery and friendship and it lives to this day. And I know now that I need to amend my mistake and mend our bond."

Merida looked toward her mother, who was hidden. The queen was gesturing to say that Merida didn't have to choose.

Merida understood at once. "I've decided to do what's right and . . . and . . . break tradition. My mother, the queen, feels in her heart that we be free to write our own story, follow our hearts, and find love in our own time."

As the crowd cheered, Merida rushed the queen to the
tapestry room. Suddenly, King Fergus threw open the door.
Merida knew her mother was in danger. "Mum! Run!"
King Fergus rushed after the bear.

Merida grabbed a needle, some thread, and the tapestry. She was sure she could break this spell. She found her brothers—who had turned into little bear cubs—and they sped toward the woods on Angus. Merida frantically sewed the torn tapestry.

King Fergus and the hunting party had caught Queen Elinor.
Lord MacGuffin led the pack. "Aye, we've got you now!"
The queen roared in terror as the king raised his sword.
But Merida suddenly burst out of the woods with
her own sword. "I'll not let you kill my mother!"

Just then, a huge beast stepped into the
Ring of Stones. His eyes gleamed evilly.

Merida gasped. "Mor'du!"

The demon bear swatted the hunters away like flies. He tossed King Fergus into the stones. Then he turned to Merida.

Queen Elinor roared. She attacked Mor'du. The bears slashed at each other, but the queen fooled Mor'du into charging a broken stone. The stone toppled over, crushing the demon bear.

Merida rushed to her mother and placed the mended tapestry over her. Nothing happened. "Oh, Mum, I'm sorry. This is all my fault. I want you back, Mum."

Queen Elinor growled softly. Merida hugged her. "I'm here for you. I'll always be here for you."

As they embraced, morning light began to fill the Ring of Stones.

Suddenly, Merida felt a human hand stroke her hair. Her mother wasn't a bear anymore! "Mum, you're fine!"

"Perfect." The queen smiled at her daughter.

The triplets came running over. They were boys again! All was right in the kingdom of DunBroch as the royal family hugged and laughed. Merida knew that from then on she could be a princess *and* still be herself.